Cook Book for Nurses

by

Sarah Chapman Hill

APPLEWOOD BOOKS
Bedford, Massachusetts

Cook Book for Nurses

was originally published in

1911

ISBN: 978-1-4290-9016-2

Thank you for purchasing an Applewood book.
Applewood reprints America's lively classics—
books from the past that are still of interest
to the modern reader.
For a free copy of
a catalog of our
bestselling
books,
write
to us at:
Applewood Books
Box 365
Bedford, MA 01730
or visit us on the web at:
For cookbooks: foodsville.com
For our complete catalog: awb.com

Prepared for publishing by HP

A COOK BOOK
FOR NURSES

BY SARAH C. HILL
FORMERLY
INSTRUCTOR IN COOKING
MICHAEL REESE HOSPITAL
CHICAGO

FOURTH EDITION
REVISED

WHITCOMB & BARROWS
BOSTON 1911

THOMAS TODD CO., PRINTERS
14 BEACON ST., BOSTON, MASS.

DEDICATED TO

MR. ISAAC GREENSFELDER

IN APPRECIATION OF HIS CONSTANT INTEREST

IN THE DIET SCHOOL OF THE MICHAEL REESE HOSPITAL

TO WHICH, FOR SO MANY YEARS, HE HAS BEEN

AN UNTIRING FRIEND

PREFACE

A word of apology seems necessary in adding another cook book to the many admirable ones already upon the market. It has long seemed to the author that much might be done in condensing recipes. She has not been able to find a book which seemed to bring together clearly enough recipes for dishes identical in method of cooking and differing in only one or two ingredients.

An attempt to accomplish this, and at the same time to offer to nurses a collection of recipes in small enough compass for their already crowded grips, is the excuse for " A Cook Book for Nurses."

CONTENTS

TABLE OF ABBREVIATIONS

c.   = cup.
tsp. = teaspoon.
tbsp. = tablespoon.

MEASURES

All measurements in these recipes are level.

QUANTITIES

1 c. = $\frac{1}{2}$ pt. = 8 ozs. = 16 tbsps. = 48 tsps.
The quantities given are sufficient for one person.

CHAPTER I

FLUID DIET

Fluid Diet includes : —

1. Milk.
   Broths.
   Beef juice.
   Beef tea.
   Tea.
   Coffee.
   Cocoa.
   Fruit beverages.
   Barley and Rice waters.
   Toast water.
   Albumen drink.

2. Gruels.
   Milk soups.

MILK PREPARATIONS

To Sterilize Milk: Utensils: If a milk sterilizer is not convenient, have a pail with tight-fitting cover. Have a hole made in the cover. Insert in the hole a cork, and through the cork put a glass thermometer so that the temperature may be ascertained without removing the lid. Put in the bottom of the pail an inverted pie plate. Use glass bottles with flat bottoms unless a rack is at hand, when rounded bottoms are practicable.

Method: Sterilize the bottles by boiling 20 minutes. Fill them nearly full of milk. Plug with sterile absorbent cotton. Set them on the plate ; fill the pail with sufficient cold water to come above the milk. Bring slowly to boiling point (212° F. or 100° C.). Boil 20 minutes. Cool as quickly as possible by plung-

ing the bottles into warm water for a few minutes until bottles
are cooled, then surround with ice water.

Pasteurisation: The utensils and method for pasteurizing
milk are the same as for sterilizing, except that the water is
brought to 170° F. or 76° C. instead of to the boiling point.

KOUMYSS

> Milk, 1 qt.
>
> Yeast, ⅕ cake.
>
> Sugar, 1½ tbsps.

Have ready bottles and corks that have been thoroughly
cleansed and boiled. If convenient, use bottles having patent
stoppers. Pasteurize the milk, then reduce temperature to 80° F.
Dissolve the yeast cake in ¼ c. lukewarm boiled water. Add to
the milk with the sugar. Pour into the bottles, filling them to
within two inches of the top. Cork tightly and tie the corks
down with strong twine. Shake well. Let stand in warm place
6 hours, then put on ice for 24 hours.

PEPTONIZED MILK

> Milk, 1 pt.
>
> Boiled water, 1 gill.
>
> Peptonizing powder, 1 (pancreatin, 5 grains; sodium bicarbonate, 15 grains).

Mix the powder and water; put in clean glass jar or bottle with
cover; add the milk. Adjust cover. Shake well. Set in water
bath of 115° F. for 10 minutes. Put immediately on ice.

MILK PUNCH

> Liquor (whisky, brandy, or rum), 1 tbsp.
>
> Sugar, 2 tbsps.
>
> Finely chopped ice, 2 tbsps.
>
> Cream or rich milk, ⅔ c.

Use a glass jar with tight-fitting cap and rubber band. Put
liquor, sugar, and ice in jar. Shake well; add the milk or cream.
Shake hard until very frothy. Serve in glasses.

EGGNOGS

	Egg	Sugar	Fluid	Flavor
PLAIN.	1	¾ tbsp.	¾ c. milk or cream.	1 tbsp. brandy.
COFFEE.	1	1½ tbsps.	6 tbsps. milk or cream.	6 tbsps. strong coffee.
w. FRUIT.	1	2 tbsps.	¼ c. water. ¼ c. chopped ice.	2 tbsps. fruit juice.

Method I: Beat egg well. Add sugar, beat again. Add remaining ingredients. Serve very cold in glass. This is the preferable method for fruit eggnogs.

Method II: Beat yolk of egg until thick and lemon-colored. Add sugar, beat again. Beat white of egg to a stiff froth, mix with the yolk and sugar. Add milk, then coffee or liquor or fruit juice. Serve in glass.

Method III: Beat yolk of egg until thick and lemon-colored. Add the sugar, beat again. Add the liquid ingredients. Pour into glass and lay on top the stiffly beaten white.

WHEYS

	Milk	Coagulating Agent
WINE.	1 c.	½ c. wine.
LEMON.	1 c.	2 tbsps. lemon juice.
RENNET.	1 c.	1 tsp. liquid rennet or ¼ junket tablet crushed in ¼ tbsp. lukewarm water.

Warm milk; when rennet is to be used, care must be taken that temperature of milk does not go above 105° F. Add coagulating agent. Let stand in warm place until a firm curd is formed. This takes about 30 minutes. Strain through double piece of cheese cloth.

WHEY FOR INFANT FEEDING

If whey is to be used for infant feeding, that obtained from rennet must be used, and the whey must be heated to 150° F. before adding it to cream. Otherwise the mixture will curdle when warmed at feeding time.

BROTHS

	Meat	Cold water
BEEF.	1 lb., cut in small pieces.	¾ qt.
MUTTON.	1 lb., freed from all fat and skin, then cut in small pieces.	1 qt.
CHICKEN.	2 lbs.	1 qt.

Clean, disjoint, remove flesh from bones, cut in small pieces. Pound the bones until well broken.

Put prepared meat in saucepan, add the cold water, bring slowly to boiling point. Simmer 4 hours. Strain into jar or earthen bowl. When cool put in ice box. When wanted for use carefully remove the fat with a spoon. If all cannot be removed in this way, pass soft paper lightly over the surface of the broth until every particle of fat is absorbed. Add salt, using ¼ tsp. to every c. broth. Heat carefully, but do not let it boil. Serve in heated bowl or cup. To vary the flavor, cook a few pieces of celery or of parsley, or 1 tsp. of any herb, or 1 tbsp. of any grain, or ½ tbsp. tapioca with the meat and water.

VEAL AND CHICKEN JELLY

Fowl, 2 lbs.
Veal knuckle, 1 lb.
Cold water, 1½ qts.

Prepare chicken as for chicken broth. Have the veal knuckle well cracked. Put them on together with the cold water. Simmer until reduced to 1½ pts. Strain through cheese cloth, season with salt, pour into small molds. When cold remove fat, unmold and serve, or reheat at serving time and serve as broth.

BROTH WITH EGG

Beat the yolk of 1 egg, or 1 whole egg, in a bowl. Pour on gradually ¾ c. hot broth. Serve at once; or, after adding egg, cook over hot water until it thickens slightly. Serve immediately or it will curdle.

OYSTER OR CLAM BROTH

Oysters or clams, ¾ c.

Milk or water, ¾ c.

Pass fingers gently over oysters to remove shell. Chop, put in saucepan with cold water or milk. Bring slowly to boiling point, but do not let it boil. Strain through cheese cloth. Salt to taste.

CLAM BROTH

Clams in shell, 6.

Cold water, ½ c.

Scrub shells thoroughly. Put in saucepan with cold water. Cook until the shells open. Strain the liquor through cheese cloth folded double. Reheat, taking care not to let it boil. Add hot cream, 1 tbsp. if desired. Pour into heated cup or bowl. Or the scalded cream may be omitted and a spoonful of whipped cream added after it has been poured into cup. Serve hot.

BEEF JUICE

Steak cut from top of round (1 lb. should yield 4 ozs.).

Beef juice press, or fruit press, or vegetable press, or old-fashioned lemon squeezer, or large piece of cheese cloth folded double and used after the manner of a stoup. (The fruit press is especially recommended where beef juice is needed in large quantities.)

Method I: Cut steak in small pieces, discarding all the fat. Thoroughly heat the press in hot water, then drain. Put the meat in a dry pan. Shake over fire until thoroughly hot but not cooked. Put at once into press. Squeeze out all the juice possible. More juice will usually be obtained by heating meat and press a second time.

Method II: Heat the press as in Method I. Trim the fat from the steak, put on broiler and sear on both sides. Cut in small pieces and squeeze as in preceding method. Where much beef juice is to be obtained, Method I is preferable.

Method III: Prepare meat as in Method I. Put in double boiler with 1 tsp. salt. Cover. Have water in lower part of boiler at a temperature of 130° F. Put boiler on back of stove, and keep it for 2 hours at such heat that the hand can bear to rest on the cover at any time during the process. A quantity of juice will be obtained by the heat, and more will be extracted by pressure.

BEEF TEA

Round steak, 1 lb.
Cold water, 1 pt.

Use a glass jar with close-fitting band and cover. Cut meat in small pieces, discarding all the fat. Put in jar with the cold water; cover tightly. Put jar on a trivet in saucepan of water at 140° F. Keep at that temperature for 2 hours. Pour off the liquid. Cool. Remove fat. Season with salt. Heat to 130° F. Serve in hot cup.

TEA

Use only an earthen, china, or enamel teapot. Scald teapot with boiling water. Pour off this water. Put in pot 1 tsp. tea. Pour in 1 c. freshly boiling water. Steep 3 to 5 minutes. Pour through strainer into cup. Serve with lump sugar and cream, or thin slices of lemon.

ICED TEA

Make 1 c. tea. Cool. Pour in glass, add lemon juice and sugar to taste, and 1 tbsp. chopped ice.

COFFEE I

Ground coffee, 2 tbsps.
White of egg, 1 tsp.
Boiling water, ¾ c.
Boiled water, ¼ c.

Mix coffee and egg with 1 tbsp. cold water in small coffee pot. Add boiling water. Boil 3 minutes. Stir down and add ¼ c.

water that has boiled, but is a little below boiling point. Let stand 15 minutes where it will keep hot but not boil. Strain and serve with lump sugar, cream or hot milk.

NOTE.— Always use coffee pot of a size proportionate to the amount of coffee needed.

COFFEE II

Have two small Florence (chemical glass) flasks, a glass funnel to fit flasks, and filter paper. Fit filter paper in funnel, put funnel in one of the flasks. Put 2 tbsps. finely ground coffee in the filter, pour over it slowly 1 c. boiling water. When it has filtered through, remove funnel to other flask to drip. If coffee is wanted stronger, pour through filter into other flask. Serve as in Coffee I.

COCOA

Cocoa, 2 tsps.
Sugar, 1 tsp.
Boiling water, ½ c.
Scalded milk, ½ c.

Mix together cocoa and sugar. Add the boiling water slowly. Boil 3 minutes. Add the milk. Beat with Dover egg beater to prevent formation of skin. Serve at once with or without whipped cream. The cocoa may be poured while hot over a well beaten egg, or over the yolk of an egg.

FRUIT BEVERAGES

General Directions: The water used in making fruit beverages should be boiled, then cooled. The fruit juices should be strained. The beverages should be served ice cold. If purity of ice supply is doubted, a good way of serving is to set the glass containing the drink in a glass or bowl filled with chopped ice. Syrup is a better sweetener than sugar. It may be made in large quantities and bottled for use.

SYRUP

Sugar, 1 c.
Water, 1 c.

Put sugar in saucepan, add water, stir until dissolved. I
12 minutes; bottle and cool.

LEMONADE AND ORANGEADE

	Water	Flavor	Sweetening
PLAIN.	¾ c.	Juice 1 lemon.	2 tbsps. syrup, 2 tbsps. sugar.
EFFERVESCING.	¾ c. Cold, but not iced.	Juice 1 lemon.	1 tbsp. sugar.

At serving time put glass containing lem
ade on a plate. Add ¼ tsp. soda bicarbon
Drink while effervescing.

EGG.　　　　　See fruit eggnog, page 3.

	Water	Flavor	Sweetening
ORANGEADE No. 1.	½ c.	Juice 1 orange.	2 tbsps. syr
ORANGEADE No. 2.		Juice 1 orange.	1½ tbsps. syr

Put 2 tbsps. cracked ice in small glass. *A*
orange juice and syrup. Serve at once.

Method I: Squeeze fruit juice into glass. Add syrup, tl
water.

Method II (if no syrup is at hand): Put sugar in bowl, *ε*
¾ c. boiling water. Stir till sugar is dissolved. Squeeze f
juice into glass; add the sugar and water. Chill.

A few thin shavings of the yellow lemon or orange rind bo
with the water or the syrup give a pleasant flavor.

Any other fruit juice may be substituted for the lemon
orange juice, varying the amount of sweetening with the acio
of the fruit.

ELLY WATER

Jelly (preferably grape or currant), 2 tbsps.
Boiling water, ¾ c.

Beat jelly with a fork until smooth. Add boiling water.
weeten to taste with sugar or syrup, and if jelly lacks flavor
dd lemon juice to taste.

ARLEY OR RICE WATER I

Barley or Rice flour, ½ tbsp.
Boiling water, 1 c.
Salt, ¼ tsp.

Mix flour and salt to a paste with a little cold water in top
f double boiler. Add the boiling water, stirring all the time.
oil 5 minutes; put over boiling water and cook 15 minutes
nger, stirring frequently. Strain. If desired, it may be flavored
ith a little lemon juice or a few raisins, or a small piece of
nnamon may be boiled with it. These should be omitted if
e water is to be used for patients suffering from intestinal
sturbances.

ARLEY OR RICE WATER II

Barley, 2 tbsps.: or rice, 3 tbsps.
Boiling water, 1 qt.
Salt, 1 tsp.

Have the water boiling in a saucepan, wash the grain, add
the water. Boil the rice water 30 minutes; the barley water
hour. Strain. Serve as in I.

OAST WATER

Toast, 2 slices well browned and *very* dry.
Boiling water, 1 c.

Break the toast in small pieces in a bowl, add the boiling
ater. Let stand 1 hour. Strain. Season with salt. If desired,
ld 1 or 2 tbsps. cream.

ALBUMEN DRINK

	White of egg	Liquid
PLAIN.	1	Water, ½ c.
MILK.	1	Milk, ½ c.
FRUIT.	1	Juice of 1 lemon or 1 orange.

Put white of egg and the chosen liquid in clean glass jar with tight-fitting cap and rubber band. Shake hard until well mixed. Strain into glass.

NOTE 1.— When fruit juice is used, sweeten to taste.

NOTE 2.— The albumen water may be flavored with lemon juice and slightly sweetened.

FLAXSEED TEA

Flaxseed, 2 tbsps.

Boiling water, 2 c.

Lemon juice, 2 tbsps.

Sugar to taste.

Wash the flaxseed. Add to the boiling water. Simmer 1 hour. Strain. Add lemon juice and sugar. Serve hot or cold.

IRISH MOSS LEMONADE

Irish moss, ¼ c.

Cold water, 1 pt.

Juice 1 lemon.

Soak moss 15 minutes in enough cold water to cover it. Remove moss, add the pint of cold water. Cook in double boiler 20 minutes. Strain. Sweeten to taste. Add lemon juice. Serve hot.

MULLED WINE

Boiling water, ½ c.

Stick cinnamon, ¼ inch.

Whole cloves, 2.

Sherry wine, ½ c.

Egg, 1.

Sugar, 1½ tbsps.

Boil water, cloves, and cinnamon 5 minutes. While boiling beat the egg and sugar well together in a small bowl. To the spiced water add the wine. Bring to the boiling point. Pour slowly over the egg and sugar, beating all the while. Serve hot.

GRUELS

Flour	Salt	Boiling water	Milk (scalded)
Barley flour, 1 tbsp.	¼ tsp.	½ c.	½ c.
Rice flour, 1 tbsp.	¼ tsp.	½ c.	½ c.
Farina, 1 tbsp.	¼ tsp.	½ c.	½ c.
Oat flour, 1 tbsp.	¼ tsp.	½ c.	½ c.
Cracker crumbs, 2 tbsps.	¼ tsp.	½ c.	½ c.

Method I: In top of double boiler mix the flour with cold water enough to form a paste. Add the boiling water. Boil 2 or 3 minutes, then set over lower part of double boiler to cook for 15 minutes, stirring frequently. Add the salt and scalded milk, and serve in a hot cup or bowl. The cracker gruel does not need to be mixed with the cold water nor cooked over hot water, but is sufficiently cooked by the 2 or 3 minutes' boiling.

Method II: Prepare any cereal by directions given on page 16, using half the quantity of dry cereal. When cooked and while hot rub through a strainer, and add ½ c. hot milk or cream.

Variations: Any one of these gruels may be varied as follows :

(1) Scald 6 raisins with the milk.

(2) Add a small quantity of lemon juice and sugar at serving time.

(3) Grate nutmeg over top at serving time.

(4) Break an egg into the serving bowl, using the whole egg or only the white or yolk as desired; beat well, pour into it the hot gruel.

(5) Scald raisins with milk, add gruel to egg as in (4), add a grating of lemon rind and of nutmeg, and 1 tbsp. each sugar and sherry. This variation makes **CAUDLE**.

(6) Cracker gruel may be varied by toasting the crackers well before rolling. Graham crackers make an excellent gruel.

OATMEAL GRUEL

Oatmeal, ⅓ c.

Cold water, 1 pt.

Salt, ¼ tsp.

Roll and pound the oatmeal on a board with a rolling pin. When floury put in a bowl and pour over it ⅓ pt. water. Let it settle. When the water looks milky strain it into a saucepan. Repeat until the pint of water has been used. Boil the oatmeal water 30 minutes, stirring frequently. Season with salt to taste, and, if necessary, dilute with hot cream or milk to desired consistency.

MILK SOUPS

The following white sauce is the foundation of milk soups :—

WHITE SAUCE

Butter, flour, milk. (The amount of each varies with the kind of soup, and is given in the table.)

Method I : Melt the butter. When bubbling add the flour and cook them together, stirring all the time until they are smooth and thick. Add the milk ⅓ at a time, stirring after adding each portion until the sauce has thickened. Add the special ingredient and seasoning.

Method II : Scald the milk. Mix the flour with cold milk sufficient to form a smooth paste. Add hot milk slowly, stirring all the time. Return to double boiler and cook 20 minutes, stirring constantly until it thickens, after that occasionally. Add the special ingredient and seasonings, and, when ready to serve, the butter broken in small pieces.

	White sauce	Special ingredient
1. CREAM OF ASPARAGUS.	Butter, 1 tbsp. Flour, 1 tbsp. Milk, ½ c.	Canned asparagus, 8 stalks. Drain from liquor. Add ½ c. fresh water. Heat thoroughly, straining out all the juice. Add to white sauce.

Salt and pepper to taste.

	White sauce	Special ingredient
2. CREAM OF CELERY.	Butter, ¾ tbsp. Flour, ¾ tbsp. Milk, 1 c.	3 sticks celery, washed, cut in small pieces and cooked with the milk for the white sauce 20 minutes in double boiler.
2a, p. 14.	Salt and pepper to taste.	

	White sauce	Special ingredient
3. CREAM OF CHICKEN.	Butter, 1 tbsp. Flour, 1 tbsp. Milk, ½ c.	½ c. strong chicken broth. Remove carefully every particle of fat. Heat before adding to sauce.
	Salt and pepper to taste.	

	White sauce	Special ingredient
4. CREAM OF CLAM.	Butter, 1 tbsp. Flour, 1 tbsp. Milk, ½ c.	½ c. clam broth.
	Pepper to taste.	

	White sauce	Special ingredient
5. CREAM OF CORN.	Butter, 1 tbsp. Flour, 1 tbsp. Milk, ½ c.	½ c. canned corn, chopped, heated 20 minutes in ½ c. water. Strain. Press out all the juice possible. Add to sauce.
	Salt and pepper to taste.	

	White sauce	Special ingredient
6. CREAM OF GREEN PEAS.	Butter, ½ tbsp. Flour, ½ tbsp. Milk, ½ c.	½ c. canned peas drained, reheated in ½ c. cold water and rubbed through sieve.
	Salt and pepper to taste. A sprig of mint may be cooked with peas.	

	White sauce	Special ingredient
7. CREAM OF ONION.	Butter, ¾ tbsp. Flour, ¾ tbsp. Milk, 1 c.	1 onion cut up and scalded with milk for white sauce.
	Salt and pepper to taste.	

	White sauce	Special ingredient
8. CREAM OF POTATO.	Butter, ½ tbsp. Flour, ½ tbsp. Milk, ¾ c.	Hot riced potato, ¼ c. Boil potato, put through ricer, add the white sauce slowly.

Salt and pepper to taste. At serving time add ½ tsp. tomato catsup or 1 tsp. chopped parsley. ¼ slice onion may be scalded with milk, then strained out.

	White sauce	Special ingredient
9. CREAM OF TOMATO.	Butter, 1 tbsp. Flour, 1 tbsp. Milk, ½ c.	½ c. stewed and strained tomato. Add $\frac{1}{16}$ tsp. soda bicarbonate before adding to white sauce.

Salt and pepper to taste. Small piece bay leaf, 1 clove, small piece onion may be cooked with tomato.

	White sauce	Special ingredient
2a. CREAM OF CELERY.	Butter, 1 tbsp. Flour, 1 tbsp. Milk, ½ c.	3 sticks celery, washed and cut in small pieces. Cook 20 minutes in 1½ c. water. Drain, pressing out all the water. Use ½ c. of this water.

NOTE. — Cream or chicken broth may be substituted for all or part of the milk in any of the above recipes.

Additional Recipes

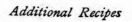

Additional Recipes

Additional Recipes

Additional Recipes

Additional Recipes

Additional Recipes

CHAPTER II

LIGHT SOFT DIET

Light Soft Diet comprises everything included in Fluid Diet 1 and 2.

Broths and soup with grains.

Eggs, poached and boiled.

Cereals.

Toasts.

Custards.

Farinaceous puddings.

Jellies.

Junkets.

Ice cream.

Ices.

BROTH WITH GRAINS

Broth, 1½ c.

Rice, barley, or tapioca, 1½ tsps.

If barley or tapioca be used soak 2 hours in cold water. Add to broth from which fat has been removed, boil 5 minutes, cook in double boiler 1¼ hours. Season with salt.

EGGS

General Principle: As albumin coagulates at 160° F., and as it toughens when boiled, eggs should be cooked below the boiling point to insure a tender consistency.

BOILED EGG

Method I: Put 1 pt. of water in a saucepan. When it boils remove saucepan to side of range, put in 1 washed egg, and let it stand from 5 to 10 minutes, according to consistency desired. Serve in heated egg cup.

Method II: Wash 1 egg and put in saucepan with 1 pt. of cold water. Bring just to boiling point. Remove from water, and serve in heated egg cup.

POACHED EGG

1 egg.
Toast.
Parsley.
Salt.

Have a shallow pan full of boiling water. Break into it 1 egg. Remove pan to place on range where water will not boil, and let it stand until the white is coagulated and a thin film is formed over the yolk. Lay a neatly trimmed piece of toast on a skimmer, dip it in the hot water to soften it, place in center of· hot plate, remove egg carefully with skimmer, place on the toast. Garnish with parsley.

CEREALS

Dry cereal	Salt	Boiling water	Time
Oatmeal, ¼ c.	¼ tsp.	1 c.	3 hrs.
Rolled oats, ⅓ c.	¼ tsp.	1 c.	1 hr.
Hominy, ¼ c.	¼ tsp.	1 c.	2 hrs.
Corn meal, ¼ c.	¼ tsp.	1 c.	2 hrs.
Farina, 3 tbsps.	¼ tsp.	1 c.	½ hr.

The farina may be mixed to a paste with cold water, and the boiling water added to it.

Patent preparations are prepared according to directions on package. They are usually improved by doubling the given time of cooking.

General Method: To boiling water in top of double boiler, add salt, then dry cereal slowly, stirring all the while. Boil 5 minutes, then put over lower part of boiler. Steam remainder of time given in table.

BOILED RICE

Rice, 3 tbsps.

Salt, ½ tsp.

Boiling water, 2½ c.

Wash rice. Add salt to rapidly boiling water; add rice. Boil uncovered from 20 to 30 minutes, until rice is perfectly soft, stirring frequently with fork to prevent rice sticking to saucepan.

STEAMED RICE

Rice, 3 tbsps.

Salt, ½ tsp.

Boiling water, 1 c.

Wash rice. Add salt to rapidly boiling water in top of double boiler. Add rice, boil 5 minutes. Put over lower part of boiler, cook 45 minutes, when water should be all absorbed.

NOTE. — The rice may be boiled in ½ c. boiling water, ½ c. hot milk to be added when it is put over hot water.

TOASTS

DRY

Cut bread in slices ¼ inch thick, cut off the crusts. Place in toaster, dry thoroughly on each side by holding at some distance from the fire, then hold closer to flame, and let it brown delicately and evenly on each side. Place on hot plate. Serve at once.

BUTTERED

Make dry toast. Butter as soon as brown, place on hot plate, cover, and serve at once.

MILK

Milk, 1 c.

Salt, ¼ tsp.

Dry toast, 2 slices.

Scald milk, add salt. While it is scalding make toast (butter toast, if desired), cut in strips, arrange them log-cabin-wise in hot

TOASTS — Continued

bowl, pour over them the milk. Serve at once. Cream may be substituted for the milk.

WATER

Make toast, 2 slices. With skimmer or fork dip them quickly in shallow pan of boiling salted water. Butter, and serve at once on hot plate, covered.

CREAMED

Make dry toast, 2 slices. Make 1 c. white sauce (page 12), using butter and flour, each 1½ tbsp. to milk 1 c. Season with salt. Dip each piece of toast quickly in boiling water, place on hot plate. Pour sauce over them. Serve at once.

This may be varied by substituting chicken broth for one-half the milk, or by using ½ c. tomato neutralized with soda ($\frac{1}{16}$ tsp.) in place of one-half the milk.

SOFT CUSTARDS

	Milk	Egg	Sugar	Flavor
PLAIN.	⅔ c.	1 yolk.	1 tbsp.	½ tsp. vanilla, or ½ tsp. wine, or a peach leaf scalded with milk, or ¼ inch piece vanilla bean scalded with milk.

	Milk	Egg	Sugar	Flavor
CHOCOLATE.	⅔ c.	1 yolk.	2 tbsps.	1 tbsp. scraped chocolate.

Melt the chocolate over hot water, add to it a small quantity of the scalded milk. Stir until perfectly smooth, then add sufficient of the milk to make of consistency to pour. Add to remainder of milk. Add to egg, and finish as directed.

	Milk	Egg	Sugar	Flavor
COCOA.	⅔ c.	1 yolk.	4 tsps.	2 tsps. cocoa.

Add sugar to cocoa. Add 1 tbsp. boiling water. Boil 1 minute. Add the scalded milk. Proceed as for plain custard.

	Milk	Egg	Sugar	Flavor
COFFEE.	⅔ c.	1 yolk.	1½ tbsps.	½ tbsp. ground coffee.

Scald coffee with milk. Strain through cheese
cloth, add to egg. Finish as directed below.

General Method: Scald the milk in a double boiler; while it
is scalding beat the egg slightly. Add the sugar to the egg,
mix. Add the scalded milk slowly to the egg, stirring all the
time. Return to double boiler and cook, stirring all the time
until it thickens. Remove from fire at once, cool quickly by
placing upper part of double boiler in cold water. When cool,
add salt and flavoring, if the latter is an extract. If not, follow
directions under special recipe. Serve in punch glass.

NOTE. — If custard should curdle, the result of over cooking, add to it at once
1 tbsp. cold milk, and pour with force into pitcher, then back again into boiler, then
into pitcher, repeating until custard is smooth.

MERINGUES FOR GARNISHING CUSTARDS

1. Beat white of egg to a stiff froth. Add 1 tbsp. powdered
sugar. Place on tin wet with cold water, place in moderately hot
oven until lightly browned and firm to the touch.

2. Beat 2 tbsps. currant or grape jelly until soft. Beat the
white of one egg stiff. Add the jelly and beat together until
thoroughly mixed.

BAKED CUSTARDS

	Milk	Egg	Sugar	Flavor
PLAIN.	½ c.	1 yolk or from ½ to 1 whole egg.	1 tbsp.	½ tsp. vanilla or grating of nutmeg.
CHOCOLATE.	½ c.	1 yolk.	1½ tbsps.	1 tbsp. scraped chocolate.

Melt the chocolate over hot water. Dilute with
scalded milk until of consistency to pour. Add to
egg. Finish as directed.

	Milk	Egg	Sugar	Flavor
COCOA.	½ c.	½ to 1 egg.	1 tsp.	2 tsps. cocoa.

Mix cocoa with the sugar. Add 2 tsps. cold

water ; mix to a paste.   Add 1 tbsp. boiling water.
Boil 1 minute, add the hot milk, and proceed as
directed.

	Milk	Egg	Sugar	Flavor
COFFEE.	½ c.	1 yolk, or ½ to 1 whole egg.	1½ tsps.	1 tbsp. ground coffee.

Scald coffee 10 minutes in the milk.   Strain
through cheese cloth.   Add to egg, and finish as
directed.

	Milk	Egg	Sugar	Flavor
RENVERSÉE.	½ c.	1	1 tsp.	10 drops vanilla, 2 tsps. sugar.

Stir the 2 tsps. sugar over fire until melted
and brown.   Pour into baking dish, then pour in
the custard mixture made from the remaining ingredients.   Unmold at serving time ; the caramel
will form a coating and sauce.

General Method: Scald the milk.   While scalding beat the
egg.   Add to it the sugar.   Mix well.   Add the scalded milk
slowly, stirring all the while.   Pour into baking dish, put it in a
pan of hot water, and bake until custard is firm.   Test by insert-
ing point of knife in center.   If clean, custard is done.

FARINACEOUS PUDDING

	Farinaceous material	Milk	Egg	Sugar	Flavor
PLAIN.	1 tbsp. corn-starch, or 1½ tbsps. farina, or 2 tsps. arrow-root.	½ c. (scalded).	½ the white of 1 egg.	½ tbsp.	Few drops vanilla, or 1 tsp. brandy, or a few thin shavings of lemon rind cooked with milk and then strained.

NOTE.— This amount of arrowroot will not make of sufficient stiffness to mold,
but the arrowroot is more delicate unmolded.

	Farinaceous material	Milk	Egg	Sugar	Flavor
CHOCOLATE.	Same as for plain.	½ c.	½ the white of 1 egg.	1 tbsp.	⅜ square chocolate melted.

Method: Mix farinaceous material, sugar, and a few grains of salt together. Add enough cold water to form a smooth, thick paste. Add to this the scalded milk. Return to double boiler and cook until it thickens, stirring all the time. Cook 10 minutes longer, stirring occasionally. Beat the egg white to a stiff froth; add the hot, thickened milk gradually, beating all the while. Pour into mold, first dipped in cold water. Chill. Unmold and serve with soft custard made from yolk of egg.

Variations: (1) After the pudding has cooked 10 minutes, pour it over the yolk of the egg beaten slightly. Put in oven for 10 minutes. Beat the white to a stiff froth, add 1 tbsp. sugar, spread it over the pudding, and return to oven to brown the meringue slightly. Serve cold.

(2) Before molding the pudding, garnish bottom of mold with a candied cherry, or serve with fruit sauce (page 22); or when unmolded make a small hollow in top of pudding, in which put 1 tsp. currant or grape jelly.

TAPIOCA PUDDINGS

	Tapioca	Fluid	Sugar	Egg	Flavor
CREAM.	2 tbsps. minute or 1 tbsp. pearl.	½ c. milk.	1 tbsp.	½	A few thin shavings of lemon rind scalded with the milk, or ½ tsp. vanilla.
BAKED.	1 tbsp. minute or pearl.	½ c. milk.	1 tbsp.	½ yolk.	A few thin shavings of lemon rind scalded with the milk, or ½ tsp. vanilla.
COFFEE.	2 tbsps. minute or 1 tbsp. pearl.	½ c. strong coffee.	2 tbsps.	½ the white of 1 egg.	

	Tapioca	Fluid	Sugar	Flavor
FRUIT.	2 tbsps. pearl or 3 tbsps. minute.	1 c. boiling water.	To taste.	1 apple or 1 peach or ¼ c. berries.

The apple may be pared and cored, or may be cut in eighths. Peaches peeled and cut in halves or eighths.

If pearl tapioca is used, soak 1 hour or longer in cold water. If minute tapioca is used, no soaking is required. Put tapioca in liquid in double boiler. Cook until transparent. (The time will be shorter in using minute tapioca than with pearl tapioca.) Add the egg yolk, and unless to be baked return to double boiler and cook until slightly thickened. Add white beaten stiff; put in mold. When cold unmold, and serve with cream or fruit sauce. If to be baked, add the cooked tapioca to the egg or to the fruit. Put in oven and cook until egg is set or fruit is soft. Where egg is used, bake in pan of hot water, as baked custard. These proportions give a pudding that will unmold when cold. If a creamy consistency is desired, use ½ the quantity of tapioca.

FRUIT SAUCE

Fruit juice (of stewed or raw fruit), 3 tbsps.
Arrowroot, ½ tsp.
Cold water, 1 tsp.

Mix arrowroot to smooth paste with the cold water. Bring fruit juice to boiling point. Add it to the arrowroot slowly. Return to fire. Boil 2 minutes.

JELLIES

The basis for all the following jellies is : —
1 tsp. granulated gelatin soaked in 1 tbsp. cold water.

	Hot liquid	Sugar	Flavor
LEMON.	6½ tbsps. boiling water.	3 tbsps.	1½ tbsps. lemon juice.
ORANGE.	4 tbsps. boiling water.	2½ tbsps.	3½ tbsps. orange juice. ½ tbsp. lemon juice.

	Hot liquid	Sugar	Flavor
WINE.	5 tbsps. boiling water.	2½ tbsps.	3 tbsps. wine. ½ tbsp. lemon juice.
COFFEE.	4 tbsps. boiling water.	1 tbsp.	4 tbsps. strong coffee.
GRAPE FRUIT.	4 tbsps. boiling water.	2½ tbsps.	4 tbsps. grape fruit juice.
IVORY CREAM.	3 tbsps. scalded milk.	1 tbsp.	6 tbsps. cold cream. ¼ tsp. vanilla.
SPANISH CREAM.	Custard made of ½ c. milk and yolk 1 egg.	1 tbsp.	White of 1 egg beaten stiff. ¾ tsp. sherry; few drops vanilla.
COFFEE CREAM.	Custard made of ½ c. milk with which 1 tbsp. ground coffee has been scalded and then strained, and yolk of 1 egg.	1½ tbsps.	White 1 egg beaten stiff.

Method: Soak gelatin in cold water 2 minutes, add hot liquid, stir until gelatin is entirely dissolved. Add flavor, strain (except Spanish and coffee creams) into mold wet with cold water. Set in cold place to harden. When jellied, unmold and serve with whipped cream.

To Serve: Orange jelly is attractive served in basket made by cutting a section of orange from either side stem end, so as to form a handle. Scoop out carefully all the orange pulp and juice, taking care not to break through skin. Strain through cheese cloth; use the juice in making the jelly. When hard, cut in cubes and fill the basket.

Or, cut small slice from top of orange with teaspoon. Remove carefully all the pulp and juice, being careful not to break the skin. Strain through cheese cloth; use the juice in making an orange jelly. Strain into orange skin. When hard, cut in quarters and arrange on plate, garnishing with green leaves or whipped cream.

Or, pour orange jelly into mold lined with sections of orange pulp. Wine or lemon jelly may be poured into small glasses to harden, reserving ¼ of quantity and filling glasses ¾ full. When jelly in glass has hardened, beat the reserved ¼ to a froth and put on top to resemble a glass of beer.

To Decorate Jellies: Pour into mold just enough liquid jelly to cover the bottom. Let this harden. Place on it, in any design fancied, small pieces of orange, or candied cherry and angelica, or Crème de Menthe cherry, or pieces of strawberry or other fresh fruit. Add a few drops of liquid jelly, taking care not to use enough to float the decorations. Let this harden, then fill the mold with liquid jelly. Let stand in cold place to harden. Serve.

Variations: —

ITALIAN CREAM.
Beat orange, lemon, or wine jelly until frothy. Mold and serve.

SPONGES.
Make a wine, coffee, or fruit jelly, slightly increasing the amount of sugar. When set, beat with egg beater until frothy. Beat white of 1 egg until stiff enough to drop. Mold, chill, and serve with custard made from yolk of the egg.

JUNKET

	Milk	Rennet	Sugar	Flavor
PLAIN.	½ c.	½ tsp. liquid rennet or ¼ junket tablet.	½ tbsp.	Nutmeg or 1 tsp. brandy.
COFFEE.	7 tbsps.	½ tsp. liquid rennet or ¼ junket tablet.	1 tbsp.	1 tbsp. strong coffee.

Heat milk to 100° F. Add sugar and flavoring. Add the rennet; stir just enough to mix thoroughly. Pour at once into serving dish, and let it stand in a warm place, in front of range, for example, until jellied. Put at once on ice. Serve cold. Where nutmeg is used, it may be grated over the junket at serving time.

ICE CREAM

	Cream	Sugar	Flavor
VANILLA.	½ c.	1½ tbsps.	1 tsp. vanilla, or ¼ tsp. vanilla and ¾ tsp. sherry.
CHOCOLATE.	½ c.	2 tbsps.	2 tbsps. grated chocolate. Melt. Add the cream gradually.

Method I: To cream add sugar and vanilla. Freeze.

Method II: Scald ½ the cream, add the sugar, stir until dissolved. Whip the remaining cream until frothy. Add the scalded cream (cooled) and freeze.

Method III: Whip the cream, add sugar and flavorings. Freeze.

Method IV: Custard. Make custard with ¼ c. milk, ½ the yolk of 1 egg, and 1½ tbsps. sugar. When cool, add ¼ c. cream, plain or whipped, and 1 tsp. vanilla. Freeze.

To Freeze Ices and Creams: Use 3 measures of ice to 1 of salt. (Rock salt should be used.) If a patent freezer is used, scald the can and paddle, then cool. Put in the cream, fasten the can in place in the freezer, put in 3 measures of ice, 1 of salt, repeating till tub is filled to just below seam of can; turn crank slowly and steadily till mixture is frozen. Remove dasher, scrape cream from sides of can, beat thoroughly, cover, and let stand at least ½ hour to ripen. If a small patent freezer is not available, creams and ices may be satisfactorily frozen by using a cocoa or baking powder tin. Scald and cool as directed above. Put in the mixture to be frozen, cover, put the can in a lard pail or saucepan. Pack with salt and ice as directed above. Every 10 minutes remove cover from can. Scrape frozen cream from sides of tin towards center, beat well. Repeat until cream is frozen throughout.

To Serve Creams and Ices: Serve on cold plates or in small glass sherbet cups. Ices may be garnished with whipped cream.

ICES

	Water	Sugar	Fruit juice
LEMON.	½ c.	¼ c.	1½ tbsps. lemon juice.

	Water	Sugar	Fruit juice
ORANGE.	½ c.	¼ c.	¼ c. orange juice.

Boil sugar and water 10 minutes. Cool. Add fruit juice. Freeze. The orange ice is attractive served in an orange basket as directed under orange jelly (page 23).

CRANBERRY ICE

Cranberries, 1 c.
Water, 1 c.
Sugar, ½ c.
Juice of ¼ lemon.

Cook cranberries in the water until soft. Strain; add sugar; cook until that is dissolved; cool, add lemon juice and freeze. Serve in glasses with whipped cream.

Additional Recipes

Additional Recipes

Additional Recipes

Additional Recipes

Additional Recipes

Additional Recipes

CHAPTER III

SOFT OR CONVALESCENT DIET

Everything included in Fluid and Light Soft Diets. In addition : —

Sweetbreads.
Calves' brains.
Fish.
Chicken.
Squabs.
Eggs in all forms except the hard-boiled whites.
Potatoes in all forms except fried.
Asparagus.
Peas.
Cauliflower.
Fruits.
Desserts, excepting pastries and rich cakes.
Occasionally chops and steaks are allowed.

MEATS, FISH, SWEETBREADS, POULTRY, BIRDS, BACON

To Select: Meats should be firm fleshed. The red meats bright in color. Fat of mutton should be white; fat of beef yellowish. Poultry should be plump in proportion to its weight. The end of breast bone in young chicken is soft and flexible. Squabs should have soft, pliable feet and bills. Fish should have firm flesh, bright, unsunken eyes, red gills. All fish and meat should be wiped with a damp cloth before cooking.

Special Preparation: Sweetbreads should be thrown into cold water for 1 hour when received from market, then drained. Put on the fire a saucepan full of water, with 1 tbsp. each salt and vinegar. When it boils, add sweetbreads. Simmer 15 to 20 minutes, drain, throw into cold water. Cool quickly. Remove membrane, fat, and veins.

Preparation of Calves' Brains: Soak one set of brains in cold water 1 hour. Remove membrane. Have ready a saucepan full of boiling salted water; add 1 tbsp. vinegar; throw in the brains and simmer for 20 minutes. Throw into cold water. At serving time break up the brains with a fork, put a small piece of butter in a pan; when melted, add the brains and stir until thoroughly heated. Season with salt. Serve at once.

Preparation of Birds for Broiling: Remove head and crop, singe, split down middle of back, remove contents, cut off feet and tips of wings. Wipe thoroughly with damp cheese cloth.

Preparation of Birds for Roasting: Remove head and crop, singe, make small cut below end of breast bone, with finger remove contents; cut off feet, wipe inside and out. Skewer into shape with toothpicks.

NOTE.—Directions for squab in following tables to be used for other birds, changing time as necessary. Dark meat (snipe, grouse, reedbird, quail, duck) should be served rare; white meat (partridge, pheasants) well done.

BROILING: When coal fire is used, heat broiler over clear fire, grease lightly, put in meat, hold close to coals on each side until seared, then holding farther away cook required time, as in table, turning every time 10 is slowly counted. Put on hot plate, spread with soft butter, season with salt and pepper. Serve at once.

If gas is used, put meat under flame and cook required time, turning but once when meat is half done.

TABLE

Meat	Time	Special directions
Steak.	1 in. thick, 8–10 min. 1½ in. thick, 10–15 min.	Garnish with parsley or cress.
Chop.	10–12 min.	Garnish with parsley or cress. Peas also an appropriate garnish.

Meat	Time	Special directions
Squab.	12 min.	Serve on toast garnished with currant jelly, peas, cress, or parsley.
Chicken.	20–30 min.	Prepare as directed for broiled squab. Cook all but 5 min. of the time with flesh side toward flame, then turn and cook skin side. The skin burns easily. Garnish with toast points and cress or parsley.
Sweetbreads.	10 min.	Split lengthwise. Brush each side with butter when half cooked. Serve with peas.
Fish.	5–20 min., according to size. Fish is done when flesh separates easily from bone.	Small fish may be broiled whole. Large fish are split or cut in cutlets. Spread large fish with butter when cooking is half done. Garnish with lemon and parsley.

ROASTING: Prepare meat, put in hot oven until surface is seared, reduce heat and cook required time, basting frequently.

TABLE

Meat	Time	Special directions
Squab.	20 min.	Serve on toast. Garnish with jelly, peas, and parsley or cress.

Meat	Time	Special directions
Sweetbreads parboiled (p. 27).	10 min.	Roll in beaten egg or melted butter, then in bread crumbs. Put in buttered pan, bake until brown. Serve with white sauce, made with 1 tbsp. each butter and flour to ½ c. milk. Garnish with peas.

To SMOTHER : In bottom of casserole, or (if that is not at hand) any baking dish that has a cover and may be used for serving, put a layer of vegetable, using either celery finely cut or a mixture of celery, onion, and parsley, or celery and carrot parboiled 5 minutes. Fill the dish half full of hot water. Put in meat to be smothered (see directions below). Cover. Cook in moderate oven required time. Serve in same dish; garnish, if desired, with peas or asparagus tips.

Gravy: If a gravy is desired, pour off the broth into a cup and add sufficient hot water to make ½ c. In small saucepan cook ¾ tbsp. butter until brown, add ¾ tbsp. flour, cook together until brown. Add liquid ⅓ at a time, stirring each time until it thickens. Season with salt and pepper and pour over meat in casserole.

Meat	Time	Note
Sweetbread. Parboil (p. 27).	20 min.	Put a small piece of butter on sweetbread when put in casserole.
Squab. Prepare as for roasting (p. 28).	30 min. to 45 min.	If desired, omit water and place strips of bacon across' breast and legs. A few juniper berries may be put in body. Brown bird in small amount of butter in frying pan before putting in casserole.

BONED SQUAB

Remove crop and head. Singe, cut off wings close to body. Cut off feet. Cut to bone the entire length of spine. Beginning at neck and working towards breast bone, scrape all the flesh away from the bone, cutting when tendonous portions are reached. When both sides have been scraped, scrape along edge of breast bone, taking care not to break through skin. Scrape flesh from leg bones, turning leg inside out as you do it. Scrape flesh from lower part of back. Holding flesh in one hand and carcass in other, pull apart. Turn legs right side out, sprinkle with salt and pepper, put edges of back together and plump into shape. Scrub large potato and cut in half lengthwise. Scrape out enough potato from each side to make a place for the boned bird. Put in the bird, tie the potato together with strong twine. Place in hot oven. Bake 45 to 50 minutes. Remove string, tie with ribbon, garnish with parsley, and serve.

JELLIED CHICKEN

Gelatin, ½ tsp.
Cold water, 1 tbsp.
Strong chicken broth, 4 tbsps.
Chopped cooked chicken, 2 tbsps.

Soak the gelatin in cold water 5 minutes. Heat the chicken broth to boiling point and pour over the gelatin. Stir until the gelatin is dissolved. Season with salt. Wet a mold in cold water, and in it pour sufficient of the gelatin mixture to just coat the bottom. Set on ice to harden. When hard, place on it 1 slice hard boiled egg, or 1 slice lemon, or any decoration preferred. Add a few drops gelatin mixture, but not enough to cover the decoration. When this is hard, mix the remainder of the gelatin with the chopped chicken and fill the mold. Unmold at serving time, and serve garnished with lettuce or cress and radishes cut in fancy shapes.

BACON BROILED

Put thin strips of bacon in broiler. Place broiler over baking pan. Cook in hot oven until crisp.

BACON FRIED

Heat frying pan very hot. Put in strips of thinly sliced bacon. As fat is drawn out, pour it into a cup; cook bacon until crisp and brown. Drain on soft paper.

BROILED HAM

Cut in moderately thick slices. If very salt, soak in hot water 15 minutes. Broil from 8 to 12 minutes. Broiled ham is more delicate when a slice of boiled, instead of raw, ham is used. Broil until browned on both sides.

CREAMED DISHES

¼ c. white sauce (made with ½ tbsp. each butter and flour to ¼ c. milk) to any one of the following : —

SWEETBREADS. ½ c. sweetbread, parboiled, cut in small pieces.

CHICKEN. ½ c. cold cooked chicken cut in small cubes. Season with salt and pepper. With chicken, chicken broth may replace part of the milk in making the sauce.

FISH. ½ c. cold cooked fish, the skin and bones removed and the flesh flaked with a fork. Season with salt, pepper, and lemon juice.

To Serve : 1. Serve on toast, garnish with parsley.

2. *Scalloped:* Put in small baking dish. Cover with dried bread crumbs ; dot with small pieces of butter ; brown in oven.

3. *With Egg:* Spread toast with creamed chicken or sweetbread. Make a depression in center. Place in that the yolk of an egg ; put in oven to set the egg.

3*a.* Add to mixture the slightly beaten yolk of 1 egg. Cook 1 minute. Serve on toast.

4. *Molded:* Use ¼ instead of ½ c. sauce to 1 c. meat or fish. Place in mold slightly buttered. Put in pan of hot water in moderate oven until firm. Unmold, garnish with parsley (and lemon if fish), pour around it 2 tbsps. sauce.

4*a*. *Pâté:* Press mashed potato that is rather stiff in a buttered pie plate, having it ¾ inch in thickness. When cold, cut out 2 rounds with a large cutter, place 1 round on a buttered tin. From center of other round cut a round with a smaller cutter. Place the ring on first round and place the small round on the tin. Brush ring and small round with yolk of egg slightly beaten. Put in oven. When browned, place pâté on hot plate, scoop a little of the potato from center, fill with creamed meat or fish. Place small round on top for a cover, garnish with parsley or peas.

4*b*. *Bread Pâté:* Cut a piece of bread 3 inches thick. Trim away the crusts, cut out the center, leaving a floor and walls ¼ inch thick. Brush with butter, place in oven to brown and dry. Fill with creamed meat or fish, and garnish with parsley.

OYSTERS

Oysters are in season from September until May.

RAW

Allow 6 to 8 for one person. Serve in deep half of shell. Arrange on soup plate filled with cracked ice, garnish (1) with quarter of lemon and parsley. (2) Make a lemon basket, according to directions for orange basket (page 23); remove all pulp from under handle, but leave half of the pulp in lower part of basket. Fill other half basket with catsup or horse-radish. Place in center of plate, garnish with parsley or water cress.

CREAMED

Wash oysters as follows : —

Put in strainer, pour over them ½ c. cold water. Pass fingers gently over each oyster to make sure it is free from shell and sand. To every cup oysters drained thoroughly from liquor, add ½ c. white sauce, made with 1½ tbsps. each butter and flour, and ½ c. milk. Heat thoroughly, and serve at once on toast, or in a bread box, or in a potato pâté. Some finely cut celery may be sprinkled over top.

OYSTERS — Continued

SCALLOPED

Wash 12 oysters. Cover bottom of individual baking dish with soft bread crumbs, moisten with 1 tsp. cream. Add 6 oysters. Cover these with soft crumbs, sprinkle with salt and pepper and 1 tsp. cream. Add remaining oysters. Cover with crumbs. Dot with butter, and bake 15 to 20 minutes. Serve at once.

PANNED

Heat small frying pan. Make 2 slices of toast. In frying pan put 5 or 6 oysters. Shake over moderate fire until edges curl. Sprinkle with salt and pepper. Add ½ tbsp. butter. Pour over 1 slice toast, garnish with parsley, lemon, and toast points. Serve at once.

BROILED

Fine bread crumbs, melted butter, 4 large oysters. With silver fork lift each oyster by tough muscle, and dip first in butter then in crumbs. Place on oyster broiler slightly greased and broil, turning often over clear fire until brown and the juices begin to flow. Serve at once; garnish with lemon and parsley.

EGGS

BOILED and POACHED (pages 15 and 16).

SCRAMBLED

(1) Beat 1 egg slightly. Season with salt and pepper. Add 1 tbsp. milk. (*a*) In small frying pan put 1 tsp. butter. When hot, add egg mixture. Stir with fork on side of range until just coagulated. Serve at once on toast. Garnish with parsley. (*b*) Pour egg mixture in top part of small double boiler. Put on the stove over hot water. Stir constantly until coagulated. Add ½ tsp. butter, and serve on hot plate. Garnish with parsley.

(2) Beat yolk of 1 egg slightly; add salt, pepper, and 1 tbsp. milk. Add white beaten stiff, cook either by method (*a*) or (*b*).

Variations: Scrambled eggs may be varied by serving on 1 slice creamed toast or by using 1 tbsp. stewed and strained tomatoes in place of the milk.

EGGS — Continued

SHIRRED

Butter slightly an egg shirrer. Break into it 1 egg. Dust with salt and pepper. Put in pan of hot water and cook in moderate oven until just coagulated. Serve in shirrer.

Variations: (1) Before putting egg in shirrer, cover bottom of shirrer with soft crumbs or with 1 tbsp. white sauce or 1 tbsp. stewed tomato or 1 slice tomato. Add the egg, and cover with same ingredient or leave plain, as desired.

(2) Instead of using an egg shirrer, scoop out all the center from a tomato or a green pepper. Break into it 1 egg, put in moderate oven until egg is just coagulated.

(3) Poach an egg. Have ready in egg shirrer 1 tbsp. white sauce. Place on this the poached egg. Cover with sauce, sprinkle with buttered crumbs, and brown in the oven. If desired, 1½ tsps. grated cheese may be mixed with crumbs.

IN NEST

(1) With a large cutter stamp out a round from a slice of bread. Toast it. Separate the white and yolk of an egg, being careful not to break the yolk. Add ¼ tsp. salt to the white, and beat stiff. Moisten toast with hot water; place it on a buttered tin; pile on it the white. Make a depression in center of white with a teaspoon, drop into it the yolk, and bake in moderate oven until firm to touch and slightly browned. Serve at once on hot plate.

(2) Separate white and yolk of egg, taking care not to break the yolk. Add ¼ tsp. salt to white. Beat stiff; put in glass or in a pretty china bowl. Place on trivet in saucepan of hot water. Place over moderate fire. As egg rises in glass, make depression in center, and in it drop the yolk. When water boils, egg is cooked. Serve in the glass.

TIMBALE

Beat 1 egg slightly, or until a spoonful can be taken up without stringing. Add salt and pepper to taste and ¼ c. milk. Strain into a small mold or cup. Set in a pan of hot water and

EGGS — Continued

bake in moderate oven until firm (about 20 minutes).   Unmold, and serve with white sauce to which has been added sufficient catsup to give a pink color.   Garnish with parsley.

OMELETS

    1 egg.

    1 tbsp. milk or water.

    Salt and pepper to taste.

    ½ tbsp. butter.

Beat yolk until thick and lemon-colored.   Add milk, salt, and pepper.   Beat white until stiff.   Fold into yolk.   Heat small frying pan.   Put in the butter, and when hot pour in the omelet. Shake over moderate fire until underside is a delicate brown, then place in moderate oven until top is firm to gentle touch. Crease through center of omelet at right angles to pan handle, tipping the pan; roll one-half the omelet over the other, guiding with palette knife.   Put a hot plate over pan and turn upside down.   Garnish with parsley.   Serve at once.

French Method: Beat 2 yolks and the white of 1 egg with a fork until a spoonful can be taken up.   Season with salt and pepper.   Add 1 tbsp. milk or water.   Heat omelet pan, put in ¼ tbsp. butter.   When hot, pour in the omelet mixture.   Shake pan over moderate fire, pricking or lifting up the egg with a fork as it coagulates, that the uncooked portion may run under.   When almost all the egg is cooked, let the underside become a delicate brown.   Tipping the pan, guide with palette knife one-half the omelet over the other half.   Hold a hot plate over pan.   Turn upside down.   Serve garnished with parsley.

NOTE. — In making omelets have a pan proportionate in size to the number of eggs to be used.

SAVORY OMELETS

Variations: (1) Mix 1 tbsp. chopped parsley with yolk of egg before cooking.

(2) Before folding, spread lower half of omelet with 1 tbsp. creamed chicken, or 1 tbsp. stewed tomato, or 1 tbsp. jelly, or

EGGS — Continued

1 tomato peeled and sliced, or 1 tbsp. asparagus tips, or 1 tbsp. peas.

(3) After omelet is turned out on plate, surround with peas or asparagus tips or creamed cauliflower or stewed tomato.

SWEET OMELETS

(4) Omit pepper, add 1 tbsp. sugar to egg.   Spread with jelly or fruit before turning.   If fruit is to be used, 1 tbsp. fruit juice may be substituted for the milk.

(5) Add 3 tbsps. warm cereal of any kind to the yolk, and omit the milk or water.

(6) Soak 2 tbsps. stale bread crumbs in 2 tbsps. milk until crumbs have taken up milk.   Then add to yolk in place of milk or water.

EGG VERMICELLI, OR JAPANESE EGGS

½ c. white sauce, made with ¾ tbsp. each butter and flour to ½ c. milk; 1 hard boiled egg, 1 slice toast or ½ c. boiled rice.

(*a*) Chop the egg white very fine, add to sauce, and heat over hot water.   Season to taste with salt and pepper.   Pour it over the toast.   Rub the yolk through a strainer or vegetable press over the sauce.   Garnish with parsley, and serve.

(*b*) In place of toast arrange the rice in form of a nest on a hot plate.   Put the sauce in the hollow, cover it with yolk, garnish with parsley, and serve.   The white of egg may be omitted in either recipe and only the yolk used.

POTATOES

BOILED

Scrub 1 potato thoroughly.   Pare or not, as desired.   In the spring, when potatoes are old, soak in cold water for 2 hours. Put in boiling salted water, cover, and boil until soft (20 to 30 minutes).   Drain thoroughly, return saucepan to warm place on range, and let stand, uncovered, until moisture has escaped.   Serve in hot dish with butter.

POTATOES — Continued

RICED

1 boiled potato. When ready to serve, press through vegetable press on a hot plate, or press through vegetable press into a baking dish. Put in hot oven to brown.

MASHED

1 boiled potato. When ready to serve, mash in same saucepan with fork or wire potato masher, or put through vegetable press. Season to taste with salt and pepper, and add sufficient hot milk to make of consistency desired. Beat until light, and pile lightly on hot dish. Or, put into baking dish, brush top lightly with 1 tsp. yolk of egg beaten with 1 tsp. milk; put in hot oven to brown. Or, fold into the mashed potato beaten light ½ the white of an egg beaten stiff. Put in baking dish; put in moderate oven, and bake until firm to touch and browned. Serve in same dish.

BAKED

Scrub 1 potato thoroughly. Put in hot oven, and bake until soft to pressure. Break skin slightly that steam may escape. Serve at once.

STUFFED

Bake 1 potato. When done, cut out a square piece from side with teaspoon. Remove all the potato, leaving skin intact. Put through vegetable press, add salt and pepper to taste, and 1 to 2 tbsps. hot milk. Beat until smooth and creamy. Add ½ the white of 1 egg beaten very stiff. Refill potato skin, heaping the potato at the opening. Return to oven to brown. Or, omit the egg white, refill potato skin, brush with ½ tsp. egg yolk beaten in ½ tsp. milk. Return to oven to brown.

CREAMED

1 boiled potato. While still hot, cut into cubes. Have ready ½ c. white sauce, made with ¾ tbsp. each butter and flour to ½ c. milk. Add ⅔ c. of the potato cubes, mixing lightly with fork to avoid breaking the potatoes. Sprinkle with chopped parsley, and serve in hot dish.

POTATOES — Continued

SCALLOPED

Put creamed potatoes in baking dish, cover with dried bread crumbs, dot with butter, and place in hot oven to brown.

FRANCONIA OR BRABANT

Pare 1 potato, parboil 10 minutes in boiling salted water. Put in buttered pan; put in hot oven and bake 20 to 25 minutes, basting three times with 2 tsps. melted butter, or baste with drippings from roasting beef.

GREEN VEGETABLES

General Rule: Wash. Cook uncovered in boiling salted water until soft. Drain immediately. If not to be used at once, chill with cold water. Reheat at serving time in butter or sauce.

See special directions for spinach.

	Time	Special directions
ASPARAGUS.	20 to 30 minutes.	Snap off stalk, tie in bunches.

Serve on toast moistened with the water in which asparagus was cooked. Pour over it melted butter, or mix with white sauce. Or serve in bread box.

	Time	Special directions
CAULIFLOWER.	20 to 30 minutes.	Soak head downward in cold water 30 minutes.

Serve with butter, salt, and pepper, or separate into flowerets. Arrange in serving dish. Pour over it white sauce. Or, mix with ½ c. white sauce; put in baking dish; cover with crumbs. Bake until brown.

	Time	Special directions
CELERY.	20 to 30 minutes.	Scrape celery. Cut stalks in ½ inch pieces.

To 1 c. celery add ½ c. white sauce, made with 1 tbsp. each butter and flour, ¼ c. water in which celery was cooked, and ¼ c. milk.

	Time	Special directions
PEAS.	20 to 60 minutes.	Shell, soak in cold water 30 minutes. S k i m undeveloped peas from top. A sprig of mint may be boiled with peas.

Season with butter, salt, and pepper. Use as garnish for meat, or serve in vegetable dish or in croustade, or mix peas with white sauce.

	Time	Special directions
STRING BEANS.	30 to 60 minutes.	String carefully. B r e a k each bean in 2 or 3 parts.

Serve with butter, salt, and pepper.

SPINACH. Wash thoroughly in several waters until perfectly free from grit. If young, put in saucepan without water, and let cook in its own juice until soft. If old, cook in boiling water. Drain, and serve with butter, salt, and pepper. Or, chop fine, reheat in a small quantity of thickened broth or in small quantity white sauce, press in shape on serving dish. Garnish with poached egg or slice of hard-cooked egg.

TOMATOES

RAW

Place tomato in bowl. Pour over it sufficient boiling water to cover it. Let it stand 1 minute, no longer. Remove skin. Put on ice to chill. With sharp knife cut in slices ; place on lettuce leaf.

STEWED

Wash 2 tomatoes. Cut in quarters ; put in stew pan. Cook 20 minutes. Season with salt, pepper, and butter.

SCALLOPED

Wash 1 tomato. Cut in half, remove seeds ; put a layer of soft crumbs in bottom of individual baking dish ; put on this the half tomato cut in small pieces, season with salt, pepper, butter, and sugar, if desired. Add another layer of crumbs, then the remaining tomato and seasoning, lastly crumbs. Place small pieces

TOMATOES — Continued

of butter on top, put in slow oven, and bake 20 to 30 minutes. Serve in small dish.

BROILED

Wash a tomato; cut in thick slices. Dip each slice in dried crumbs, then in beaten egg, last in crumbs; place on greased broiler and broil until brown, turning frequently.

STUFFED

Wash 1 tomato, cut thin slice from stem end. Remove seeds and pulp. Sprinkle inside of tomato with salt, and invert for 30 minutes. Melt $\frac{1}{3}$ tbsp. butter, add $1\frac{2}{3}$ tbsps. chopped cold chicken or other cold meat, $1\frac{2}{3}$ tbsps. soft bread crumbs, the tomato pulp, salt and pepper to taste. Cook 2 or 3 minutes. Add 2 tsps. beaten egg. Cook 1 minute longer. Refill tomato with mixture, place in buttered pan, sprinkle with crumbs, bake 15 minutes in hot oven.

SALADS

FRENCH DRESSING

Salt, $\frac{1}{8}$ tsp.

Pepper, a dash.

Oil, 1 tbsp.

Vinegar, $\frac{1}{3}$ tbsp.

Mix salt and pepper. Add oil slowly, then the vinegar. Beat with Dover egg beater for 1 minute.

CREAM DRESSING

Mix together in top part of double boiler the following ingredients : —

Salt, $\frac{3}{4}$ tsp.

Mustard, $\frac{3}{4}$ tsp.

Egg, 1, slightly beaten.

Butter, 2 tbsps.

Cream, $\frac{3}{4}$ c.

Add very slowly, stirring all the time, $\frac{1}{4}$ c. vinegar.

Put over hot water and cook until thickened, stirring all the time.

SALADS — Continued

MAYONNAISE

> Salt, ½ tsp.
> Mustard, ½ tsp.
> Cayenne, a dash.
> Egg, 1 yolk.
> Olive oil, ¾ c.
> Vinegar, 1 tbsp.

Mix together in bowl the salt, mustard, and cayenne. Add the yolk. Beat together with a fork. Add the oil drop by drop (a medicine dropper is a convenience), beating and stirring all the while with fork. When very thick, add 1 tsp. of the vinegar. Then add oil more rapidly than at first, but never adding at one time more than can be well incorporated. When very thick, thin with vinegar. Repeat until materials are all used. Keep in cold place. At serving time the white of 1 egg beaten stiff or ¼ c. whipped cream may be added.

SALADS WITH FRENCH DRESSING

1. Plain lettuce.

2. Lettuce and radishes. Radishes may be cut to represent flowers or in thin slices.

3. Lettuce and finely cut celery.

4. Lettuce shredded. Arrange in form of nest, filling with 2 or 3 small balls the shape and size of birds' eggs, made from Neufchâtel or cream cheese.

5. Water cress.

6. Water cress and radishes.

7. Water cress and chopped apple.

8. Water cress and thin-skinned oranges cut in thin slices. Use lemon juice in place of vinegar in dressing.

9. ½ potato cut into very fine cubes while hot, and mixed with dressing. When cold, 1 tsp. chopped onion added. Serve on lettuce leaf.

10. The same as 9, with addition of 1 or 2 tsps. chopped celery when cold.

SALADS — Continued

11. Same as 9. 1 or 2 English walnuts cut in quarters added when cold.

12. Lettuce and green peas or asparagus tips.

13. Sliced tomato and lettuce, or tomato jelly and lettuce.

SALADS WITH CREAM OR MAYONNAISE DRESSING

To MARINATE. — If mayonnaise is used, mix materials with a French dressing, and let stand 30 minutes or longer. Use the mayonnaise for masking or garnishing.

1. Finely cut celery alone or with 1 or 2 tsps. chopped apple or 1 or 2 chopped nuts. Garnish with curled celery and celery tops.

2. Celery, finely cut apple, and nuts. Serve in cups made by scooping out a red apple. Garnish with celery tops.

3. Any of the following vegetables, alone or in combination : asparagus ; young, tender beets ; young, tender carrots ; peas ; string beans. Serve on lettuce.

4. Tomato, stem end cut out. Cavity filled with dressing or with finely cut celery or chicken. Or tomato cut in quarters or sliced. Serve with lettuce or cress. Do not marinate the tomato salads.

5. 3 tbsps. chicken cut in cubes, 1½ tbsps. celery cut fine. Serve on lettuce and garnish with celery tops and olives.

6. Chicken finely cut, lettuce shredded.

7. Celery cut fine. Sections of orange pulp or grape fruit pulp. Serve in orange basket or half grape fruit skin.

TOMATO JELLY

Gelatin, 1 tsp.

Cold water, 1 tbsp.

Tomatoes, ¾ c. scant.

Small piece onion.

Small piece bay leaf.

1 clove.

⅛ tsp. salt.

Cook tomatoes with seasoning 10 minutes. Soak the gelatin in the cold water. Strain the tomatoes. Add 8 tbsps. of the liquid to the gelatin. Stir until dissolved. Pour into a mold. When set, turn out on a lettuce leaf. Serve with any salad dressing.

DESSERTS

TRIFLES

Any of the soft custards may be served by pouring while hot over a slice of stale, plain cake, previously soaked in orange juice or sherry, or by pouring when cold over 3 sections of orange pulp, or over ½ cooked or raw peach, or 1 apple baked without skin. Cover with meringue.

SPONGE CAKE CROQUETTES

Cut the crusts from a piece of stale sponge cake. Trim in shape of a croquette. Dry the crusts. Roll them fine. Moisten the cake thoroughly with cream, or wine, or fruit juice, or cream flavored with wine or fruit juice. Then roll it in the crumbs. Put in serving dishes and pour around it soft custard.

HAMBURG, EGG, OR FRUIT CREAM

Egg	Sugar	Flavor
1	1 tbsp.	1½ tbsps. lemon juice.
1	¾ tbsp.	2½ tbsps. orange juice.
1	¾ tbsp.	1½ tbsps. wine.

In top of double boiler beat egg until thick and lemon-colored. Add sugar and fruit juice, and cook until it thickens. Beat white of egg very stiff. Add the cooked mixture, mix thoroughly, turn into glass or saucer. Cool.

PRUNE JELLY

Gelatin, 1 tsp.
Cold water, 1 tbsp.
Prunes, 5.
Water in which prunes have cooked, 4 tbsps.
Sugar, 1½ tbsps.
Wine, 1 tbsp.

Wash the prunes. Add water, soak 1 hour or longer. Put on to boil in same water, and cook until stones will slip out easily. Remove stones; add sugar to prunes with 4 tbsps. of the water in which the prunes have cooked, and return to fire. Soak gelatin in cold water. When prunes and sugar come to the boiling point, add to the gelatin. When dissolved, add the wine. Pour into a mold. When set, unmold, and serve with whipped cream.

DESSERTS — Continued

PRUNE WHIP*

    Prunes, ¼ lb.

    Sugar, ¼ c.

Wash prunes, soak over night in cold water to cover. In the morning cook in same water until soft. Remove stones, and press prunes through a sieve. Add the sugar, and cook until of the consistency of marmalade. Beat white of 1 egg very stiff. To it add 3 tbsps. prune mixture and ¼ tsp. lemon juice. Put in glass dish and serve with soft custard, or pile lightly on baking dish and bake in moderate oven 8 minutes, or until firm to touch. Serve hot or cold with soft custard.

FRUIT WHIPS

Fruit	White of egg	Powdered sugar
Sliced peaches, ½ c.	½	¼ c.
Strawberries or raspberries, ½ c.	½	¼ c.

Method: Put egg white, fruit, and sugar in large bowl, and beat until stiff enough to drop. Serve cold.

APPLE SNOW

    ½ the white of 1 egg.

    Strained apple sauce, 2 tbsps.

    Lemon juice to taste.

Add lemon juice to apple sauce. Whip egg white stiff, fold in the apple sauce, pile on dish, and serve with soft custard. Garnish with cubes of currant jelly.

CHARLOTTES

Gelatin	Cold water	Thin cream scalded	Heavy cream	Sugar	Flavor
¼ tsp.	1 tbsp.	1 tbsp.	7 tbsps.	1½ tbsps.	¼ tsp. vanilla.
¼ tsp.	1 tbsp.	1 tbsp.	7 tbsps.	2½ tbsps.	1 tbsp. grated chocolate melted.

Soak gelatin in the cold water 5 minutes. Add the scalded cream, and stir over hot water until dissolved. (If chocolate is used, add the hot cream gradually to the melted chocolate, stirring

DESSERTS — Continued

all the time.) While it is cooling, whip the heavy cream stiff.
Add sugar and vanilla. Pour the gelatin, cooled but not stiffened,
in a slow stream into the whipped cream, beating all the while.
Line a mold with lady fingers split in two, or with a slice of
sponge cake; pour in the charlotte. Set in cold place to stiffen.
Unmold, and garnish with whipped cream and candied cherries.

Bavarian Cream

Gelatin, 1 tsp.
Cold water, 1 tbsp.
Hot custard, ¼ c. (made with ¼ c. milk and the yolk of 1 egg).
Sugar, ½ tbsp.
Vanilla, ¼ tsp., or 1 tbsp. chocolate, melted.
Whipped cream, ¼ c.

Method: Soak gelatin in cold water 5 minutes. Add the hot
custard and sugar. Stir until gelatin is dissolved. Flavor (if
chocolate is used, add the hot milk slowly to it before making
the custard). Set in ice water to cool, beating almost constantly
with Dover egg beater. When beginning to stiffen, fold in the
whipped cream. Pour into mold. Unmold at serving time and
serve. Garnish with whipped cream.

Ice Cream Croquettes

Make macaroon crumbs by drying a few macaroons in the oven,
then rolling them to a powder on the board with rolling pin. Remove cream, frozen very hard, from freezer, using an ice cream
scoop. Turn it out on the board and roll it in the crumbs, using
a palette knife. Place on plate, and garnish with whipped cream
and candied cherries.

FRUITS

Baked Apples

Wash 1 apple. Pare or not, as desired; core. Fill cavity
with sugar. Put in small baking pan; fill pan half full of boiling
water; put in moderate oven. Bake until soft, but do not let it
lose its shape.

FRUITS — Continued

APPLE COMPOTE

Have ready a saucepanful of boiling water. Pare and core 1 apple. Boil in the water until soft, but not broken. Remove with skimmer. To ½ of the water add 2 tbsps. sugar. Cook until reduced to 2 tbsps. Cut out a round of bread ; dip it in the syrup. Place on plate. Place on this the apple. Fill cavity with currant or other bright-colored jelly ; pour a spoonful of syrup around it. Serve with whipped cream.

PAINTED LADY

Wash 1 red apple. Boil in water to cover until soft, turning frequently. Remove from water. Peel with silver knife. Scrape away all the pulp adhering to skin and replace on apple. Smooth with knife. To ½ c. of the water add 2 tbsps. sugar, and boil until reduced to 2 tbsps. Add 1 tbsp. orange juice. Pour over apple. Serve cold.

APPLE SAUCE

(*a*) Wash 2 apples. Cut in eighths, removing core. Put in double boiler with a very small amount of water. Steam until very soft. Rub through sieve ; sweeten to taste. If the apples lack flavor, a thin slice of lemon or a couple of whole cloves may be cooked with them.

(*b*) Wash and pare 2 apples. Cut in eighths, removing core. Drop in cold water to prevent discoloration. Cook together in saucepan for 5 minutes ¼ c. sugar, and ½ c. water. Add enough of the apple slices to cover bottom of pan. Cook until soft and clear. Remove with skimmer and repeat process until all the apple is cooked. Pour the remaining syrup over them. Serve cold.

BAKED PEARS OR QUINCES

Pare and core a pear or quince. Put it in a small stone crock, fill cavity with sugar, pour in water to the depth of 2 inches. Cover crock, and put in very slow oven to cook for several hours, until fruit is perfectly soft, but without losing shape. Remove to plate, pour over it syrup from crock. Serve cold.

FRUITS — Continued

Stewed Prunes

Wash prunes, and soak in cold water to cover 24 hours. Put on to cook in same water, and cook until soft. Sweeten to taste. Cook 3 minutes longer after sugar is added.

Additional Recipes

Additional Recipes

Additional Recipes

Additional Recipes

Additional Recipes

Additional Recipes

CHAPTER IV

SPECIAL DIETS

DIABETES

The following foods are suitable in diabetes, and in all cases where starches and sugars are forbidden.

Soups

All meat broths and soups without the addition of grains.
Clam broth (page 5).
Broths with egg (page 4).
Cream soups made as directed (page 51).

Fish

All kinds. Appropriate sauces; melted butter, Hollandaise (page 52).
(Clams and oysters sometimes forbidden.)

Meat

All kinds except liver: gravies not to be thickened with flour. Use the natural meat juice.
Horse-radish sauce (page 53).

Eggs

Recipes already given, omitting bread crumbs. Extra recipes (page 53).

Vegetables

Spinach, and other greens. Lettuce, cresses, French artichokes (page 54); radishes, celery, tomatoes, cucumbers, mushrooms. Sometimes asparagus, cauliflower, egg plant, onions, and string beans are allowed.

49

DIABETES — Continued

SAUCES

Use as much butter as can be worked in.

Hollandaise sauce (page 52).

Cream salad dressing (page 41).

Mayonnaise dressing (page 42).

French dressing (page 41).

DESSERTS

Nuts (except chestnuts and peanuts). Jellies and cream puddings, sweetened with saccharin instead of sugar.

NOTE. — In using saccharin, use $\frac{1}{4}$ grain for bland desserts, $\frac{1}{2}$ grain for very acid desserts. Dissolve the saccharin in $\frac{1}{2}$ tsp. cool water, and, except where food is baked, add at the end of the cooking.

Recipes already given that may be adapted to diabetics by substituting cream for all or part of the milk, and substituting saccharin for sugar, are the following:

CUSTARDS

Baked and boiled, flavored with vanilla or grated peel of $\frac{1}{2}$ orange or lemon (pages 18, 19).

A boiled custard may be poured, when cold, over some chopped nuts.

BAVARIAN CREAM (page 46).

$\frac{1}{2}$ to 1 tbsp. chopped nuts may be added as mixture is put in mold.

CHARLOTTE RUSSE

Omit lady fingers. Line mold with sections of orange or grape fruit, or add $\frac{1}{2}$ to 1 tbsp. chopped nuts to mixture as it is put in mold. When unmolded, garnish with half nut meats.

CREAMS AND JELLIES

Ivory cream (page 23).

Spanish cream (page 23).

Ice cream flavored with vanilla or coffee, or with the addition of chopped nuts.

DIABETES — Continued

Hamburg cream (page 44).
Lemon jelly (page 22).
Orange jelly (page 22).
Grape fruit jelly (page 23).
Coffee cream (page 23).
Lemon, orange, or cranberry ice (pages 25, 26).

FRUITS

Oranges, lemons, grape fruit, sour cherries.

BREADS

Made from gluten or glutosac flour.
Gluten wafers.
Gluten Zwieback.   (Health Food Co.)
Proto puffs.   (Health Food Co.)
Bread and cakes from almond meal.

BEVERAGES

NOTE. — All beverages requiring sweetening are sweetened with saccharin in place of sugar.   See note on use of saccharin (page 50).

Tea.
Coffee.
Koumyss.
Albumenized milk, water, lemon or orange or grape fruit juice.
Lemonades.
Egg Lemonades.
Effervescing lemonades.
Eggnog made with cream instead of milk.
Coffee eggnog.

RECIPES ESPECIALLY SUITABLE TO DIABETICS

CREAM SOUP

	Liquid	Flavor	Thickening
CELERY.	1 c. cream.	3 sticks celery cut in small pieces, scalded 20 minutes with the cream.	1 or 2 egg yolks.

	Liquid	Flavor	Thickening
CHICKEN.	½ c. scalded cream.	½ c. chicken broth.	1 or 2 egg yolks.
CLAM.	½ c. scalded cream.	½ c. clam broth.	1 or 2 egg yolks.
TOMATO.	½ c. scalded cream.	½ c. stewed and strained tomato, to which add $\frac{1}{16}$ tsp. soda bicarbonate before adding to cream.	1 or 2 egg yolks.

Method: Scald the cream. Heat the flavoring to boiling point (note special direction for celery soup). Add the flavoring slowly to the hot cream. In a bowl beat slightly the egg yolk. Add the hot liquid slowly, stirring all the while. Serve at once. Or, return to double boiler and cook 1 minute, stirring constantly. Serve immediately.

SPINACH SOUP

Cooked spinach, 1 tbsp.
Broth (beef or chicken), ⅔ c.
Egg yolk, 1.
Cream, 1 tbsp.

Add broth to spinach. Cook 5 minutes, rub through sieve. In soup bowl beat yolk of egg with cream. Add the spinach and broth; return to double boiler. Cook 1 minute. Serve at once.

SAUCES

HOLLANDAISE

Egg yolk, 1.
Butter, ¼ c.
Vinegar, ¼ tbsp.
Salt, ⅛ tsp.
Pepper to taste.

Divide the butter in 3 pieces. Put 1 piece in top of double boiler with vinegar, egg yolk, salt and pepper. Place over boiling water. Stir constantly while butter melts. Add second piece of

SAUCES — Continued

butter. Stir until this is melted. Add remaining butter, continue stirring. As soon as it thickens remove from fire, and serve at once.

Vary by adding (1) 1 tbsp. grated horse-radish root; (2) ½ tsp. chopped parsley; (3) 1 tbsp. tomato purée; this is obtained by stewing and straining 1 c. tomatoes and cooking down to a thick pulp.

HORSE–RADISH

Horse-radish root, grated, ½ tbsp.
Whipping cream, 1 tbsp.
Vinegar, ¾ tsp.

Beat the cream stiff. Add salt, pepper, and the vinegar drop by drop. Fold in the horse-radish root.

CUCUMBER

Grate ¼ cucumber. Season to taste with vinegar, salt and pepper. Serve with fish.

EGGS

Use recipes already given, omitting toast, bread crumbs, and white sauce. Use the following variations in addition to those already given.

SCRAMBLED (page 34)

Add 1 tbsp. grated cheese when egg is partially cooked, or add ¼ Neufchâtel cheese just before removing egg from fire.

SHIRRED (page 35)

Butter egg shirrer, break into it an egg. Dust with salt and pepper, cover with 1 tbsp. grated cheese. Bake, set in hot water until cheese is melted and egg is cooked.

TIMBALE

Add 1 tbsp. grated cheese before pouring egg into mold. Substitute cream for all or part of the milk.

OMELETS

Mix 1 tbsp. grated cheese with yolk.

CHEESE CUSTARD

Egg, 1.
Cold water, 2 tbsps.
Cream, 4 tbsps.
Melted butter, 1 tbsp.
Grated cheese, 1 tbsp.
Salt and pepper to taste.

Beat the egg slightly, add other ingredients in order named. Pour into mold, and bake; set in pan of hot water in moderate oven until firm.

VEGETABLES

SCALLOPED TOMATOES

Butter bottom and sides of small baking dish. Cover bottom with chopped nuts. Over this put a thick layer of stewed tomatoes, sprinkle with salt and pepper, dot over it small pieces of butter; add a layer of chopped nuts, then tomatoes, salt, pepper, and butter, as before. Cover with chopped nuts. Bake in hot oven 15 minutes.

FRENCH ARTICHOKES

To prepare: cut off stem close to leaves, and remove the hardest bottom leaves. Cut off top leaves so as to leave an opening. Remove the choke. Tie the leaves in shape, and soak 30 minutes in cold water; to a saucepanful of boiling salted water add 1 tbsp. vinegar, put in the artichokes, and cook 30 to 45 minutes, or until the leaves will pull out easily. Drain, remove string, and serve with Hollandaise sauce.

SAUTÉD MUSHROOMS

Wash 6 mushrooms quickly, not allowing them to soak. Break off the stems close to the caps. Scrape them, and break each in two or three pieces. Put the caps, after peeling, in a saucepan with 1½ tbsps. butter. Cook 2 minutes; add 1½ tbsps. cream. Cook slowly until mushrooms are tender. Season with salt and paprika. Serve with beefsteak.

VEGETABLES — Continued

BROILED MUSHROOMS

Break the stems from 6 large mushrooms. Wash and peel the caps. Lay them, gills down, on a buttered broiler, broil 2 or 3 minutes, then turn and finish cooking with gills up. Sprinkle with salt and paprika, and put a small piece of butter in each cap. Serve at once on a thin piece of toasted gluten bread.

BAKED MUSHROOMS

Prepare as for broiled mushrooms. Lay them on a buttered pan gills up. Put small pieces of butter in each cap; dust with salt and paprika, bake in hot oven 10 minutes, basting twice with cream or chicken broth.

SALADS

Any of the salads already given may be used, omitting, of those with French dressing, Nos. 7, 9, 10, 11, 12, and of those with cream or mayonnaise dressing No. 2.

ADDITIONAL

Celery and cheese. Wash 3 or 4 crisp sticks of celery. Fill the hollows with either of the following mixtures. Serve as a relish, or use as a salad with French dressing.

(1) Cream 1 tbsp. butter; mix with 1 tbsp. grated cheese to form a paste. Season to taste with salt and paprika.

(2) Work together 1 tbsp. American Club House cheese and 1 tbsp. butter. Season with salt and paprika.

EGG

Boil 1 egg hard. Cut in half and remove yolk. Mash yolk, and moisten with cream or mayonnaise dressing. Refill whites, and serve on lettuce leaves.

Vary by adding to the yolk 1 tsp. chopped chicken or other meat, or 1 tbsp. grated cheese.

SPINACH

Season cold, cooked, chopped spinach with butter, lemon juice, salt and pepper. Press into a mold; trim a slice of tongue the size of the mold. Unmold the spinach on the tongue. Garnish the top of the spinach with mayonnaise, to which has been added finely chopped olives, parsley, and pickles. Garnish with parsley.

CHEESE SANDWICH

Cut two very thin slices of Swiss cheese.

(1) Butter them lightly, and spread one slice with finely chopped chicken or other meat moistened with salad dressing. Lay on this a lettuce leaf, and cover with the other slice of cheese.

(2) Spread the cheese thinly with salad dressing; lay on this the lettuce leaf. Cover with the other slice of cheese.

GLUTEN BREAD I

Water, 1 pint.
Salt, 1½ tsps.
Yeast, ½ cake.
Butter, 1 tbsp.
Gluten flour, 5 to 6 c.

Add salt to the water, and bring to 80° F. Dissolve yeast cake in ¼ c. lukewarm water, add to salt and water, add the butter; when melted add sufficient flour to knead. Knead well, put in bowl, cover, and set in warm place to rise. When double its bulk (about 3 hours) cut down, shape into loaves; put in buttered pans, let rise again until double its bulk, and bake 50 minutes with decreasing heat. If desired, add 1 c. broken nut meats to dough just before putting it in the pans.

GLUTEN BREAD II

Lukewarm water, 1 c.
Salt, ½ tsp.
Eggs, yolks and whites beaten separately, 2.
Yeast, ½ cake.
Glutosac flour, 2¼ c.

Soften the yeast in ¼ c. of the water; add to the remainder of the water. Then add the salt, the well-beaten yolks, the stiffly beaten whites, and lastly the flour. Knead slightly; put in greased bread pan; let rise to double its bulk, and bake in hot oven 40 minutes.

GLUTEN WAFERS

> Cream, 2 tbsps.
> Gluten flour, ¼ c.
> Salt, ¼ tsp.

Make a stiff dough of the flour, cream, and salt. Knead well. Roll out until as thin as paper. Cut into any shapes desired, and bake in a moderate oven 6 minutes. If desired, add 1 tbsp. finely chopped nuts to the dough.

NON-NITROGENOUS DIET USED IN NEPHRITIS

Avoid all irritating substances, as spices, pepper, mustard.

SOUP

> No meat soups. Use cream soups, pages 12–14 (except cream of green pea).
> Chicken broth.
> Chicken broth with rice.
> Clam broth.
> Vegetable soup (page 58).

CEREALS

> All kinds.

BREADS

> Stale bread, toast; zwieback.

FISH

> Occasionally.

MEATS

> White meat of chicken.

VEGETABLES

> All kinds, except peas, beans, and lentils.

NON-NITROGENOUS DIET—Continued

FRUITS
Stewed fruits.

DESSERTS
Junket. Farinaceous puddings, without eggs. Ice cream, ices, charlotte.

BEVERAGES
Milk, cocoa, weak tea.

VEGETABLE SOUP
Carrot, scrubbed, scraped, and chopped, 2 tbsps.
Turnip, scrubbed, pared, and chopped, 2 tbsps.
Celery, washed and chopped, 3 tbsps.
Potato, scrubbed, pared, and chopped, ½ c.
Onion, pared and chopped, 2 tbsps.
Butter, 2 tbsps.
Water, 1 pint.
Cook all the vegetables except the potato in the butter for 3 minutes. Add the potato, cover, and cook 3 minutes. Add the water and boil ¾ hour, or until the vegetables are thoroughly soft. Beat with a fork to break the vegetables. Season to taste with salt and pepper; add 1 tsp. parsley; serve.

DIET IN RHEUMATISM

Avoid red meats, meat soups, sweets. Eat cream soups, fish, eggs, white meats, cereals, fresh vegetables.

DIET IN LIVER DISORDERS

Avoid alcohol, highly seasoned food, strong tea and coffee, rich cheese, pastry, cake, very fat or very sweet foods. Take milk, buttermilk, junket, eggs, lean meat, sweetbreads, chicken, squab, fish (excepting those rich in fat), fresh green vegetables, salads without oil, fresh fruit

Light Soft Diet

First Day

Breakfast.	Soft cooked egg, toast, coffee.
10 A.M.	Broth with egg.
Dinner	Cream of celery soup.
	Toast cut in strips.
	Wine jelly.
3 P.M.	Cocoa, a cracker.
Supper.	Milk toast, tea.

Second Day

Breakfast.	Juice of an orange.
	Farina, toast, soft egg, coffee.
10 A.M.	Eggnog.
Dinner.	Chicken broth with rice.
	Toast.
	Soft custard.
3 P.M.	Gruel, cracker.
Supper.	Rice cooked with milk.
	Toast, tea, junket.

Third Day

Breakfast.	Cream of wheat.
	Poached egg on toast, coffee.
10 A.M.	Broth with barley.
Dinner.	Clear soup.
	Scraped beef balls on toast.
	Tapioca pudding.
3 P.M.	Cocoa with egg, zwieback.
Supper.	Cream toast.
	Orange jelly, tea.

SOFT DIET

First Day

Breakfast.   Fruit in season.
                  Oatmeal.
                  Poached egg, bacon.
                  Toast, coffee.

10 A.M.   Milk, bread and butter sandwich.

Dinner.   Cream of tomato soup.
                  Roast chicken.
                  Mashed potato, toast.
                  Vanilla ice cream.

Supper.   Creamed sweetbreads.
                  Toast, tea.
                  Baked apple.

Second Day

Breakfast.   Grape fruit.
                  Shredded wheat biscuit.
                  Broiled finnan haddie.
                  Toast, coffee.

10 A.M.   Egg lemonade, scraped beef sandwich.

Dinner.   Broth with rice.
                  Broiled squab on toast.
                  Currant jelly.
                  Stuffed potato, spinach.
                  Orange snow.

Supper.   Egg timbale, lettuce, French dressing.
                  Toast, tea.
                  Stewed prunes.

Third Day

Breakfast.   Orange.
                  Cream of wheat.
                  Omelet, roll, coffee.

10 A.M.	Egg and sherry, wafer.
Dinner.	Cream of chicken soup.
	Lamb chop, peas.
	Creamed potato.
	Bavarian cream.
Supper.	Creamed codfish on toast.
	Baked potato, toast, cocoa.
	Painted lady.

Full Diet

Breakfast.	Fruit.
	Oatmeal.
	Broiled ham.
	Roll, coffee.
Dinner.	Clear soup.
	Roast beef.
	Franconia potatoes, creamed cauliflower.
	Charlotte russe.
Supper.	Creamed chicken in potato border.
	Tomato salad, bread and butter.
	Baked apple, sponge cake, tea.

Diabetic Diet

I

Breakfast.	Grape fruit.
	Bacon, 2 poached eggs.
	Gluten bread and butter, coffee, cream, saccharin.
10 A.M.	Glass of cream.
Dinner.	Cream of celery.
	Beefsteak with mushrooms.
	Spinach and egg, broiled tomato.
	Lettuce, French dressing.
	Vanilla ice cream.

Supper.   Broiled halibut steak.
           Water cress salad.
           Gluten and nut wafers, tea.

II

Breakfast.   Orange.
              Proto puff (Health Food Co.), cream.
              Omelet.
              Coffee, cream, saccharin.

10 A.M.   Egg lemonade.

Dinner.   Cream of tomato soup.
              Roast mutton, celery.
              French artichoke, Hollandaise sauce.
              Ivory cream.

Supper.   Codfish and cream, spinach salad.
              Gluten bread and butter, tea.

III

Breakfast.   Grape fruit.
              Scrambled eggs with cheese.
              Gluten bread toasted, coffee.

Dinner.   Spinach soup.
              Roast beef, horse-radish sauce.
              Scalloped tomato, water cress.
              Orange jelly.

Supper.   Broiled squab, celery, and cheese.
              Broiled mushrooms.
              Gluten wafers, tea.

Additional Recipes

Additional Recipes

Additional Recipes

Additional Recipes

Additional Recipes

Additional Recipes

CHAPTER V

INFANT FEEDING

Use the following recipes in connection with the formulæ : —

Whey for infant feeding, page 3.

Barley water, either recipe, page 9.

Pasteurize milk and cream according to directions on page 2.

Have all utensils boiled before using. . If not convenient to use a certified per cent cream, use top milk according to the following table : —

To obtain top milk, use a siphon or a Chapin cream dipper.

Percentage of fat in top milk.   Judson & Gittings.

Fat in whole milk, 4%.

Fat in upper, $\frac{1}{5}$ or 6 oz., 16%.

Fat in upper, $\frac{1}{4}$ or 8 oz., 13%.

Fat in upper, $\frac{1}{3}$ or 11 oz., 10%.

Fat in upper, $\frac{1}{2}$ or 16 oz., 7%.

MILK FORMULÆ FOR INFANT FEEDING
(Courtesy of Dr. Isaac Abt)

I

The total amount of each formula is 24 ozs.

	Formula	16% cream	Whey	Milk sugar	Water
1.	Fat, 1.5%. Sugar, 6%. Proteid, .75%.	2$\frac{1}{4}$ ozs.	15 ozs.	$\frac{3}{4}$ oz.	6$\frac{1}{4}$ ozs.
2.	Fat, 1.75%. Sugar, 6%. Proteid, 1%.	2$\frac{1}{2}$ ozs.	14 ozs.	$\frac{3}{4}$ oz.	7$\frac{1}{2}$ ozs.
3.	Fat, 2%. Sugar, 6%. Proteid, 1.25%.	3 ozs.	18 ozs.	$\frac{3}{4}$ oz.	3 ozs.

	Formula	16% cream	Whey	Milk sugar	Water
4.	Fat, 2.5%.	3¾ ozs.	15 ozs.	¾ oz.	5¼ ozs.
	Sugar, 6%.				
	Proteid, 1.25%.				
5.	Fat, 3%.	4½ ozs.	12 ozs.	¾ oz.	7½ ozs.
	Sugar, 6%.				
	Proteid, 1.25%.				

To every ounce of the mixture ½ grain of sodium bicarbonate may be added. *Example:* To 24 ozs. of the mixture add 12 grains sodium bicarbonate.

II

The method of working out the following formulæ will be found in "Infant Feeding," by Judson & Gittings.

The diluent may be cereal water or plain water. 1 oz. of lime water or 12 grains of sodium bicarbonate may be added to each of the mixtures.

The total amount of each mixture is 24 ozs.

Age	Formula	16% cream	4% milk	Sugar	Diluent
Premature.	Fat, 1%.	1.5 ozs.		7 drs.	22.5 ozs.
	Sugar, 4%.				
	Proteid, .25%.				
1st to 4th day.	Fat, 1%.	1 oz., 3 drs.	3 drs.	1 oz.	22 ozs., 2 drs.
	Sugar, 5%.				
	Proteid, .3%.				
5th to 7th day.	Fat, 1.5%.	1.5 ozs.	1.5 ozs.	1 oz.	21 ozs.
	Sugar, 5%.				
	Proteid, .5%.				
2d week.	Fat, 2%.	2 ozs., 4 drs.	1 oz.	1 oz., 2 drs.	20.5 ozs.
	Sugar, 6%.				
	Proteid, .6%.				
3d week.	Fat, 2.5%.	3.5 ozs.	1 oz., 3 drs.	1 oz., 2 drs.	19.5 ozs.
	Sugar, 6%.				
	Proteid, .8%.				

Age	Formula	16% cream	4% milk	Sugar	Diluent
4th to 8th week.	Fat, 3%. Sugar, 6 %. Proteid, 1%.	4 ozs.	2 ozs.	1 oz., 1 dr.	18 ozs.
3d month.	Fat, 3%. Sugar, 6%. Proteid, 1.25%.	3.5 ozs.	4 ozs.	1 oz.	16.5 ozs.
4th month.	Fat, 3.5%. Sugar, 7%. Proteid, 1.5%.	4 ozs.	5 ozs.	1 oz., 2 drs.	15 ozs.
5th month.	Fat, 3.5%. Sugar, 7%. Proteid, 1.75%.	3 ozs., 5 drs.	6 ozs., 3 drs.	1 oz., 2 drs.	14 ozs.
6th to 10th month.	Fat, 4%. Sugar, 7%. Proteid, 2%.	4 ozs.	8 ozs.	1 oz., 1 dr.	12 ozs.
11th month.	Fat, 4%. Sugar, 5%. Proteid, 2.5%.	3 ozs.	12 ozs.	5 drs.	9 ozs.
12th month.	Fat, 4%. Sugar, 5%. Proteid, 3%.	2 ozs.	16 ozs.	½ oz.	6 ozs.
13th month.	Fat, 4%. Sugar, 5%. Proteid, 3.5%.	1 oz.	20 ozs.	4 drs.	3 ozs.

Additional Recipes

Additional Recipes

Additional Recipes

Additional Recipes

Additional Recipes

CHAPTER VI

Three points are to be observed in serving a tray :
First.   Cleanliness.
Second. Convenience.
Third.   Attractiveness.

CLEANLINESS.

(*a*) Be sure that tray and tray cloth are spotlessly clean ; china, glass, and silver bright and shining.

(*b*) When a tray is removed from the sick room, destroy all foods remaining on it.

ATTRACTIVENESS.

(*a*) Let size of tray be proportionate to meal to be served.

Do not use a large tray for a fluid meal. And for a convalescent's meal use a tray large enough to hold the necessary dishes without crowding.

(*b*) Do not offer too large portions. Smaller portions are more tempting, and also prevent waste. It is better to give a second portion than to overload the plate.

(*c*) Keep the rims of plates and saucers clean. Take care that in serving liquids, the parts of the bowl or glass above the level of the liquid are not streaked with it.

(*d*) In cutting bread or toast have the pieces uniform in shape and size.

(*e*) Serve hot dishes *hot*. Cold dishes *cold*, but not chilled. Do not serve lukewarm foods.

(*f*) If it can be avoided, do not use dishes of different colors.

(*g*) In garnishing dishes, let the garnish be simple.

(*h*) If flowers are available, one or two laid in the napkin are attractive, but do not use too many.

(*i*) Cover the whole tray with a napkin when carrying it from the kitchen to the patient.

CONVENIENCE.

DIAGRAM OF CONVALESCENT TRAY

1. On a breakfast tray, this should be the cereal or fruit dish; on dinner tray the soup bowl or plate; on supper tray the plate containing the principal food of the meal.

2. Knife, edge of blade towards plate.

3. Soup spoon, if needed.

4. Fork, prongs turned up. If more than one fork is needed place it here, having the fork to be used first farthest from the plate.

5. Teaspoons. Be sure to have as many as will be needed on the tray so as to avoid delay.

6. Butter chip, unless bread and butter plate is used.

7. Glass. Fill glasses only three-fourths full.

8. Salt and pepper.

9. Sugar bowl.

10. Cream pitcher.

11. Tea or coffee pot.

12. Cup and saucer. Take care that handles of teapot, cream pitcher, and cup are all turned towards outside of tray.

13. Plate of bread or toast. If a dinner tray, the plate of bread may be put over the soup bowl, and this may be the plate holding the main part of the dinner.

14. Dessert.

15. Extra vegetables, or salad.

The napkin may be put on the bread plate, and the bread put within a fold of it, or it may be put at the right of the soup spoon.

INDEX

Index

Printed in the United States
119492LV00014B/12/P